Too Many Cats

L. BECK

AuthorHouse™
1663 Liberty Drive
Bloomington, IN 47403
www.authorhouse.com
Phone: 1 (800) 839-8640

Published by AuthorHouse 07/10/2020

ISBN: 978-1-7283-6646-3 (sc)
ISBN: 978-1-7283-6647-0 (e)

authorHOUSE®

Dedication

For my sister, Rhonda Dutra, who loves her cats and my dad, Ralph Wofford, who loves his cows (and my mother).

There was a girl named Rhonda Rue, who had such affection for the creatures that mew. She pet them and praised them. She gave them such toys. She fed them and called them good girls and boys.

Rhonda Rue had a big heart, that's true. But the house she lived in was small. The fur balls she once thought were so fun now drove her up the wall!

She had to plan her every step around the paws and tails that lay in wait to detonate a round of feline wails!

And though she tried to scoop the poop and change the litter boxes, the mess and odor they produced made her feel quite nauseous.

She couldn't move. She couldn't breathe. She couldn't cook or dress or believe

such little things could multiply and make
her want to scream and cry.

So, after she had looked about, she decided to move out!

"Let the cats have the house. If they wonder where I went,
they can stick a nose outside and see I've pitched a tent."

Across the way an old man came. He shook his head and then, "Young Rhonda Rue!" he called out loud, "I'm Ralph Regimen. I've watched you carry kittens in by ones and twos and threes. I've seen you dumping litter boxes while you cough and sneeze. I've not seen you smile nor sing, nor speak with joy of anything for months since you've been bringing in the feline foes you think are friends. There simply are too many of them!

They eat you out of house and home. They work your fingers to the bone caring for their needs. What started out a single pet has turned into a grave regret and SPREAD LIKE A DISEASE!

Rhonda Rue, it's up to you to stand and take control. Find loving homes for the furry bones. Put camping in your yard on hold." And when Ralph Regimen had finished his say, he turned on his heels and walked away.

That night Rhonda Rue slept under the stars
and considered the choices she had.

The following day she gave cats away and felt a little sad.

In weeks to come much more was done and she started to feel glad. The life so complicated and small became easy and large - all because Rhonda Rue followed Ralph's advice and learned to be in charge.

She set her feet down wherever she pleased. She cooked and cleaned and dressed with ease.

Instead of thirty cats that mew, she happily shared her home with two. She had just two to love and hold.

Until there were three, when she met Woe.
Rhonda Rue married Woe Nomo'e and became
Rhonda Rue-Nomo'e. And together they managed
without regret a life of love and two little pets.

CPSIA information can be obtained
at www.ICGtesting.com
Printed in the USA
BVHW021503240720
584534BV00012B/1099